Annie's Solo Mission

by Marcy Kelman
illustrated by Aram Song
Based on the Episode written by Jeff Borkin

Disney
PRESS

New York

It was a big day for Annie. Leo was giving her flying lessons! "Today you'll learn the three most important tricks for flying Rocket," said Leo. "Are you ready?"

"Ready, big brother!" Annie said excitedly.

"Okay, here's the first lesson you'll need to master—the Up-and-Down Trick," said Leo. "If you want to make Rocket jump over something, you need to reach your arms up really high above your head and then bring them down really fast."

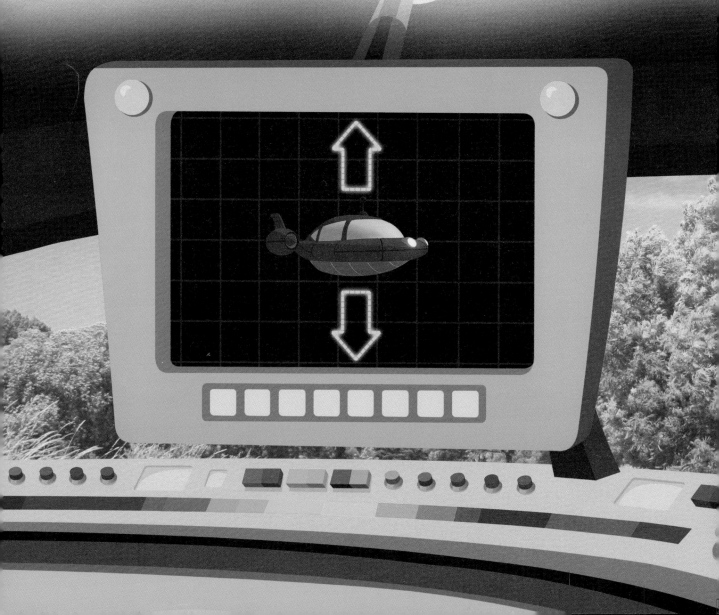

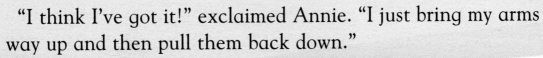

"I think I've got it!" exclaimed Annie. "I just bring my arms way up and then pull them back down."

"Great job, Pilot Annie!" Leo said, beaming.

Can you try the Up-and-Down Trick? Way to go!

"Next, you'll need to know the Squeeze Trick," explained Leo. "It comes in handy when you need to fly Rocket through a really tight space."

"Whoa, that sounds hard!" said Annie.

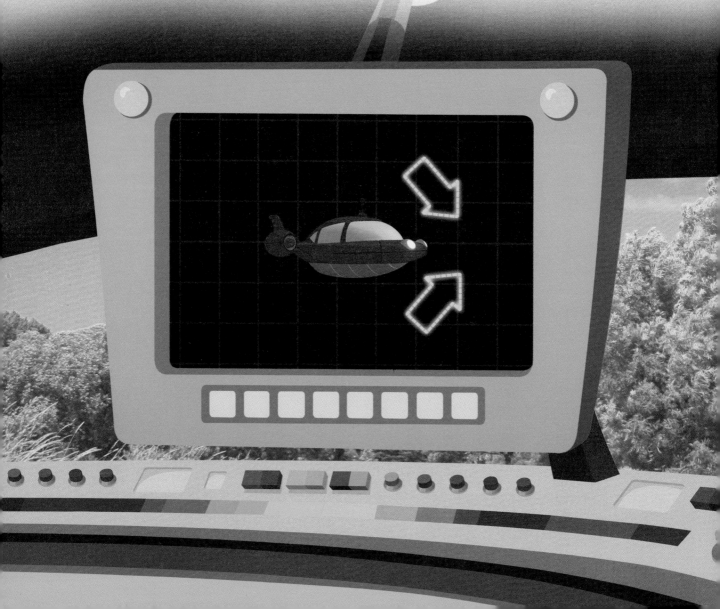

"It's actually pretty easy," said Leo. "Just cross your arms and pat your shoulders." **Pat! Pat! Pat!**
"This is fun!" Annie shouted.
Can you cross your arms and pat your shoulders? Great job!!!

After she mastered the Up-and-Down Trick and the Squeeze Trick, Annie was ready to learn the hardest move of them all— the Loop-de-Loop Maneuver!

"Okay, this one is a bit difficult," cautioned Leo. "To make Rocket do big roller-coaster loops in the air, you need to clap your hands in a circle."

After watching her brother a few times, Annie joined in and made big clapping circles in the air with him.

"Hey, I'm doing it!" laughed Annie. "I should give myself a big hand!"

Can you do the Loop-de-Loop Maneuver? Hooray!

After Annie's flying lesson, the team decided to blow some superbubbles.
Do you like to blow bubbles?
The Little Einsteins blew their superbubbles into some pretty wild shapes! *What shapes do you see?*

Annie ran to find her camera. She wanted to take pictures of the team's superbubbles before they all popped.

"I've got an idea," said June. "Let's all blow bubbles at the same time and make one humongous superbubble!"

Can you pretend you're blowing superbubbles with the Little Einsteins?

Oh, dear! June, Quincy, and Leo blew a superbubble so big that it carried all three of them away!
Annie raced back with her camera, but her friends were nowhere to be found.

"Hey, where did they go?" Annie wondered aloud. "I wanted to take their picture!"

"Up here, Annie!" shouted Quincy. "Hate to burst your bubble, but we won't be making the photo shoot anytime soon!"

"We need you to rescue us," said June. "If you fly Rocket up here, you can catch our bubble in his Bubble Wand."

Annie was nervous. "Me? But I've never flown Rocket by myself before!"

"You can do it, Annie," Leo assured her. "You're ready!"

Inside Rocket, Annie prepared for her solo mission.

"According to this flight plan, first I need to do the Up-and-Down Trick over the mountains, then perform the Squeeze Trick to fly through a small opening between two rocky cliffs, and finally do a Loop-de-Loop Maneuver through Gustav Klimt's painting *Expectation* to get to the superbubble."

However, Annie couldn't go on her mission until she figured out how many times she'd need to perform each flying trick. She needed to track down some clues!

1)

2)

3)

How many times did Annie need to perform the Up-and-Down Trick? To find out, use your finger to "pop" each bubble containing a picture that begins with a letter in the name **JUNE**.

How many bubbles still have pictures in them? Yes, three bubbles!
Annie needed to do the Up-and-Down Trick three times.

*How many times did Annie need to perform the Squeeze Trick? To find out, use your finger to "pop" each bubble containing a picture that begins with a letter in the name **QUINCY**. How many bubbles still have pictures in them?*

You're right—four bubbles! Annie needed to do the Squeeze Trick four times.

*How many times did Annie need to perform the Loop-de-Loop Maneuver? To find out, use your finger to "pop" all the bubbles containing pictures that begin with a letter in the name **LEO**. How many bubbles still have pictures in them?*

You're right—two bubbles! Annie needed to do the Loop-de-Loop Maneuver two times.

Will you help Annie perform all three flying tricks so that she can rescue her friends in the superbubble?

First, we need to perform the Up-and-Down Trick to get over the mountains. Raise your arms up and then bring them down quickly three times: **Up, down! Up, down! Up, down!**

Next, we need to do the Squeeze Trick to get through the small opening between the cliffs. Cross your arms and then give your shoulders four strong pats. **Pat! Pat! Pat! Pat!**

Finally, we need to do the Loop-de-Loop Maneuver to exit the painting. Make two big clapping circles in the air. Hooray!

"I cannot believe it!" shouted Quincy. "You flew Rocket all by yourself."

"We're so proud of you, Pilot Annie!" exclaimed June.

"Way to go, sis!" Leo beamed. "I'm bubbling over with pride!"

"Well, I think it's time for us all to *pop* back home." Annie giggled. **"Mission completion!"**